TABLE OF CONTENTS

IT'S ALL ABOUT ME

Let me introduce myself.

My full name is Mary Katherine Joan Bell, why do parents dish out names like this? Everyone calls me Katie, as Mary really does not suit me! Bell is my married name (2nd marriage) I kept the name because, it was just easier, I like the sound of Katie Bell it has a good "ring" to it ha-ha and I know it really pisses my ex off that I have kept it. In fact, I once received a very aggressive text message from one of his children demanding that I changed it! So, I am definitely keeping it!

I am in fact coming up to my 48th birthday! OMG! How did that creep up on me! I don't mind getting older in fact I kinda like it, but it worries me that I've gotten probably more than halfway through my life and don't feel like I've quite figured what it's all about yet? I have been married and divorced twice! I have three beautiful daughters, two dogs, I have been slim and overweight, currently I would say I'm a little over and erm shall we say curvy? I have battled for years with my weight and body image, but more recently I believe I have come to terms with my curves, I would love to say that God blessed me with great breast, but the truth is when I lose weight they disappear into flat sagging spaniel's ears, so there is another great excuse to eat pie! I am the true definition of marmite; people generally love me or loath me and nothing in-between! This is mainly due to my honesty, yes honesty! Everyone says they love honesty until you give them the honest answer that they don't want to hear.

I am straight talking, oftentimes my mouth engages before my brain does, I don't believe there is any point in fluffing things up or going around the houses, if you ask me a question I am going to give you the brutal truth, so if you don't really want to know if you look fat in the dress, Don't ask me!

Some would say I'm a cold hearted bitch! Others that know me would say that I am genuine, loyal, and caring!! Yes caring! I might not go in for mushy displays of affection, but if you are in my inner circle, I will walk over hot coals for you! (I have actually walked over hot coals, but that's another story)

But if you have a boggie hanging out of your nose, excessive facial hair, or body odour, I will tell you.

My Step-Mum who has in fact earnt the title of Mum because she brought me up loved and cared for me from the age of three, is a really sweet and kind soul, she always used to say to me.

"Honesty is the best policy" I think she now regrets giving me this advice, as she nearly has a nervous breakdown when I walk in the room for fear of what I might say or do.

My daughters all dread going out with me, they would describe me as a serial complainer and drama queen. I will argue this point profusely, I just know what I like, I refuse to pay for sub-standard, lukewarm food that I could absolutely cook better myself at a fraction of the cost at home. I also struggle with confined spaces and lack of daylight; I will never understand why some restaurants try to sit you on the tiniest internal table so close to others that you can in fact smell their halitosis and unfortunately, I am probably going to tell them or at least slide the

2

number of a great hygienist over.

No, no I mean why? Doesn't everyone want a big enough table, big enough to have nibbles an ice bucket and elbow room? I want to sit by the window or weather permitting outside and I want enough room between tables that you can't hear my conversation about how last night the batteries ran out on my rampant rabbit, so I had to use my sonic toothbrush, without anyone getting embarrassed.

Any way rant over, let's get back to me...

I am slightly sex obsessed a little bit crass, I drink like a sailor and I'm an outrages flirt, I flirt with everyone! Yes, male or female I am going to lick my lips, flick and twiddle my hair, fiddle with the button on my blouse, whilst holding eye contact with you until you look uncomfortable and then I will smile an enticing smile. I just can't help myself!

Flirting was something I learnt from a very young age, before my dad married my step-mum, I lived with my Dad, Grandpa and my Uncle, and we were the original three men and a baby! I assume this is why I'm often described as one of the boys as I am far more at ease in male company. I learnt how to wrap all three of these great and strong men around my little finger and they knew it.

Sometimes my flirting technique doesn't quiet work due to the fact that I'm a little on the blind side and sometimes struggle to focus, I have the ultimate resting bitch face and get lost in my own thoughts, leading to me looking like I'm going to smash your face in or indeed plotting your un-timely death, now apparently this can be a little unnerving and not at all flirtatious just plain intimidating! Well, you can't get it right every time!

PRINCESS

Earlier this year it was my eldest daughters 21st Birthday, jeez that makes me feel old, time really does fly by. Anyway, she is a total princess and expected the moon and stars with a dusting of glitter thrown in for her birthday. Now I know I have had 21 years to prep and save for this day, but not gonna lie, I didn't! Oh, go on righteous middle-class people with your fancy cars, holiday homes and savings accounts, I should have saved and prepped! But as a single working mum, that runs her own business (often not able to take a wage) I, we have had to live hand to mouth and yes, we do definitely live well beyond my meagre means! Many would call this stupid! I call it living for the moment, seizing the day creating memories filled with laughter! Every Christmas for the last eight years I haven't made my December mortgage payment because it gets spent on creating a magical day that my girls will never forget, memories and moments have to be seized and no it's not always convenient and sometimes yes its slightly irresponsible, but when my time comes to leave this world my headstone will read "lived a lot, loved even more and is still laughing" not she made every single mortgage payment on time. So as the big day was looming, I did what every irresponsible single mum would do…I got a new credit card! (Others already maxed out) I thought, what is the best present I could give? Time and memories! So, I booked us a holiday! Not just any holiday oh no no no, this was a 5-star luxury all-inclusive holiday with upgrades galore. She was going to get the full Princess treatment! This was going to cost me a fortune and I knew I would be paying it off for the next few years, but I also knew her useless shit off a dad would yet again fail her. Having not provided for any of them in any way shape or form since I kicked his sorry cheating arse out, he wasn't going to become Mr Miracle on her birthday. So as always, I must double up and make sure my princess's dreams do come true! Okay, okay I'm not all sweetness and light! I figured the holiday would go down a treat but also, it's a win, win as I get to go!

I have worked so hard the last few years and have gone without so much so that my girls never have to, also paying my staff rather than myself or even the tax man!! I know stupid but I love these people, hot coals, and all that. I deserve this holiday as much as anyone but there is no way I could have justified it for myself. Life has been a battlefield from the start. Don't get me wrong I have many beautiful memories and my Dad and step Mum did all they could to provide the best that they could, but somehow, I always managed to get myself into stupid situations and make bad decisions. One of those decisions was to marry the useless shit that became the girl's dad. The thing was he was such a charmer and so handsome. For some reason at this point in time, I felt desperate to find a man and settle down. All of my friends were in long term relationships and I was scared that I might get left on the shelf!! I look back now and want to scream at my younger self! Why was I in such a hurry? Why did I not know my self-worth? Why did I settle? The only justification I have is that my body clock was ticking so loud I thought everyone could hear it, and sadly I just thought that I was never going to find my Mr Right, so this Mr Rightnow will have to do.

We flew to the Dominican Republic to get married, around fifteen family and friends came along to witness and celebrate with us. I have to say we had the most amazing time, with so many funny incidents that I could write a whole book on that! Like when during a game o golf my younger sensitive teenage brother got a birdie! He literally go a birdie, knocked its head clean off!! He was absolutely devastated.

The night before the wedding, we had a massive row, mainly because he was being a complete dick! Showing off and trying to belittle me. ran off crying saying I wouldn't marry him, and ran straight into hi mum. His mum was and still is a lovely, kind, wise soul. I told her wha happened, and she simply said, "you shouldn't marry him". Hmmm should have listened, but I felt bad, everyone had invested time and money, not to mention fly half way round the earth to get there! And more importantly, I had a beautiful dress that I had dreamt of wearing, wanted my day as a princess.

We went ahead and needless to say it was no bed of roses, well actually it was, but those really thorny roses!.

When I was 7 months pregnant, I found out that he was having an affair, one of many as it turned out. I threw his sorry ass out.

It's a long story as baby was very poorly when she was born, but hi actions proved that I had no other option, I had to get out. So I sold th house, and ended up homeless with three under-fives for a short period of time. Thankfully a friend gave us his back bedroom until I could ge straight. He was truly an angel sent from above. From this rock bottor I re-built, I bought a house in a rather undesirable area (back when yo could get 100% mortgage) and I went back into education, got degree, re-married another not-so-great move, got divorced again! and re-built my business with many knocks along the way. Yet even thoug I have done all of this alone with three children I still can't justif spending money on a holiday for myself, why as women do, we fee like this? but as a 21st birthday gift for my princess, it somehow seem acceptable.

The holiday was all we expected and more, I'm not going to bore yo with the details of how we lavished in luxury I'm not one to gloat.

was however a dream holiday where we got absolutely spoilt and indulged by all the fabulous staff that worked there. when it came to the last day, we both felt like crying. Liv because she missed home, her boyfriend, and sisters. Me because I didn't want to go back to the harsh and hard reality that is my life.

We said our goodbyes and hugged the staff that now felt like friends, one of the bar managers said he would come and wave us off which I thought was sweet as we had barley spoken to him. We packed up our last few bits and went to check out. As soon as we got to reception, we were told that our luxury private transfer was ready and waiting, just one of the many upgrades, well who wants to travel on a coach with a load of drunken brits, no thank you. Though I had drank my fair share during the holiday, we were continuing with the pretence that we were wealthy until we land back in Manchester. With a tear in my eye, we headed off to the airport.

DUCKS IN A ROW

Have you ever had that feeling, where it seems as if the stars have aligned? Like there is a greater power controlling thing's beyond your means just to make one moment in time possible. Well, I have these all the time! Some would say it's because I'm a dreamer and I can't argue with that, but I truly believe the universe has my back and things happen for a reason even though we might not see or understand it from the off. Well, this was one of those days. We sat on the plane for 2 hours wondering what the delay could be? The pilot came out and introduced himself and explained that the plane was un-safe to fly and that it would be tomorrow evening at the earliest before the fault could be fixed. My initial reaction was thank the Lord that this had been discovered before we were in the air! followed by, oh shit what hell hole are they going to put us in? Then I hear the pilot say "we are taking you all to Jaz Aquamarine Hotel" what? OMG! Only the most beautiful hotel we had left a few hours ago!! What were the chances?

As soon as we arrived back, we decided to avoid the commotion of everyone checking in and just head straight to the bar, after all we know that the hotel is beautiful and were only staying one more night so no need to fuss and worry over what the room will be like. After 4-5 wasted hours at the airport I need a stiff drink! As we walk over to the bar, I see the friendly bar manager, I sneak up behind and shout SURPRISE! As he turns around, he went bright red, and all the other staff lean in shouting and slapping him. Apparently, he had wanted to get my number, but I had left in the private transfer before he had a chance to get my number! I mean, what were the chances of all the stars aligning to get me back to the hotel so that he could get my number? Oh yes there is a God, and he does move mountains!

MY YEAR OF YES!

Every New Year I make crap resolutions that I never keep! Be more organised, lose weight, get fit, get debt free, utilize my time better give up or at least cut back on drinking, if I'm honest I don't really want to give up drinking, I love it! It's my go to de-stressor, my friend my constant and reliable hug in a bottle, it makes me feel warm and woozy, it numbs the pain of life and gives me a confidence I just don't possess when sober. But apparently a bottle of wine a day is not socially acceptable? Which is funny because nearly all the single mums I know drink at least that. Don't get me wrong I'm no alcoholic I don't wake up craving a drink, but as soon as I get home from work it's what I want/need I suppose if I were being brutally honest, I would say I am in fact a functioning alcohol dependent that occasionally binge drinks but who needs a title?

This year I decided against making crap resolutions and instead make this my year of yes. Oh, I'm not going to say yes to everything, I have far too many sick and warped minded friends that would take advantage of that. But I am going to say yes to new adventures, doing things on my own and pushing through the comfort zone, It is so easy o say no and make excuses for why I can't or shouldn't do something, out this year is going to be different, I'm so bored of waiting for others o do things and even worse agreeing to go somewhere and then letting me down, so this year I'm just saying balls to it! I'm gonna do the things I want to do whether you join me or not.

Day three after the holiday and the holiday blues well and truly kick in. There are several reasons for this,

Mo the gorgeous bar manager has been messaging me, saying how he misses me and my beautiful eyes..... yes I know its BULLSHIT, I'm not one of these women you see in take a break magazine that sells her house to go and live with her twenty something Egyptian lover! I am not so naïve, and through the power of google translate I tell him exactly that! Cut the crap Mo I don't need to hear it. However, it Is nice to get a little attention and of course it brightens my day even though I don't believe a word of it, it still makes me smile.

Its bloody freezing!! I can't believe as I flew into Manchester airport the snow and freezing temperatures also blew in! Oh, how I hate the cold. At this point I am seriously considering selling up and moving to a warmer climate and no not Egypt before you start just Spain or somewhere that's not too far and you can get cheap flights to.

Work – today is my first day back in salon, a nice 12-hour day without breaks to ease me back in.

Oh my, just shoot me now! I'm so bored with this life! My Mum always used to say you can't run away from your problems! Just this once I would like to try! So, with all this in mind, I have decided to book a holiday back to Egypt!! ALONE!! OMG! I can't believe I'm going to do this, I can make up loads of reasons why I shouldn't, like I've not yet paid my tax bill. But I want some fun! I'm going to go absolutely crazy if I don't have some excitement in my life. I can justify this to myself and everyone else, after all I deserve some time out, some escapism. As a single mum I haven't had this in such a long time, I constantly work trying to grow a business and it's been so hard

with no other income coming in. I'm not in a relationship so I don'
even have that to escape into. No, I definitely deserve the time out
Also, the compensation money from being delayed (overnight in 5-sta
accommodation) has come in the post today and it's more than the cos
of a week's holiday! Happy days! So that's it decision made, I've
booked it!!! EEK!! What are my girls going to say? Ha-ha it's funny
how the roles have reversed.

I know that if I tell the girls they will be shocked! Shocked that I dare
do something without consulting them first and once over the shock
they will start to lecture me on how ridiculous it is to fly all the way to
Egypt with the hopes have having sex with a young, rather gorgeous
but yes much younger man.

I do how ever tell Mo that I've booked my return and he seemed
delighted by the looks of his now frequent picture messages (slightly
blushing)

I also tell my besties as they Know and understand me, all of which
said, "go for it, just don't come back pregnant!" Oh, my could you
imagine?? The thought makes me nauseous! However, I had a new coi
fitted last month so I should be safe on that front, but I suppose I bette
had get some other protection as I don't want to bring back any othe
nasty surprises.

LET THE ADVENTURE BEGIN!

I arrived at the airport feeling relatively calm, it's actually much less stressful when you're not worrying about what everyone else is doing. I have my new bright yellow bag that has compartments for all my documents, my liquids are separated into a clear bag, the iPad is loaded with films, I'm looking positively chic yet still comfortable in my blue denim button up dress with hidden side pockets (I love a dress with pockets) and my cute leopard print ankle boots with a little heal and an oversize scarf that can double as a blanket should the flight be cold, oh yes I think I have thought of everything , I smile to myself as I board the plane and order a bottle of fizz for the journey. As it turns out I have the whole row to myself! Absolute bliss. No one getting past every two mins for the toilet or annoying chit chat it's just me my films and a bottle of prosecco, well it is a six-hour journey I think I can make it last.

There were no dramas at all I sailed through security and straight into the transfer taxi and within minutes had arrived at the beautiful destination that will be my home for the next seven days.

As soon as I entered the reception several staff greeted me with smiles and hugs pleased to see I had returned so soon, I checked in and was given the gold VIP wrist band. I'm still not sure whether Mo had arranged this or whether all returning guests got them, either way I am now a VIP and I like it! I ordered a couple of large G & T's to be sent to the room, my nerves were kicking in a little bit, and I needed to calm down and compose myself, tonight I have to look good as later I will see Mo.

There is a knock at the door and there before me are two rather gorgeous men well one probably still in the boy category, the younger one had brought my suitcases, he was super cute but definitely very young, too young I laughed to myself, the other had my ice filled drinks and a smile that could melt hearts, this is going to be interesting. I don't know what it is, but I just can't help but flirt and there is something about warm holiday air that turns me into a crazy wild cat! I purr my thankyou as I see them out both of them took a second glance as I knew they would. Well let's face it the guys here are all crazy horny as no women work in the hotel and the guys do 30 days on of 15-hour days then one week off so it's unlikely they are getting much action.

I ran a bath and with loads of bubbles and relax away my nerves with the G & T and warm water lapping up against me. I look at my body through the bubbles and wonder what Mo will think about it? Over the years I have gained a few pounds, I wish I hadn't but at the same time I'm more comfortable with my curves now than I ever was when I was younger. It's crazy isn't it, when I was a size 8 with perky breast I used to sit and cry that I couldn't go out because I was so fat!!

Now as a voluptuous size 14 with pendulous breast I feel confident and sexy, though slightly concerned as to what knickers I should put on! It's the old Bridget Jones thing, do I go for the big knickers or the pretty ones? First world problems!!

I decided as this is my first night that I need to look effortlessly good without being overtly sexy, I don't want to look like I'm trying to hard (desperate) also I'm thinking nothing will happen tonight, I've only just got here, Mo will give me time to settle in. So, I opt for big knickers a cute knee length floaty dress with sleeves, disguise the bingo wings, some cute kitten heels, and a whole lot of Chanel. Mo has been messaging asking where I am, so I suppose this is it, I have my big girl pants on and I'm going to stride into that bar, alone but with confidence.

BOYS, BOYS, BOYS!

It's a little daunting walking into the bar area alone, it's a huge outdoor area with all the seats surrounding the dance floor with probably around 200 people some dancing some sat drinking and chatting, as I walk I feel like all eyes are on me, I know in reality hardly anyone has bat an eyelid but I feel slightly sick and very afraid that I'm probably gonna go arse over tit in front of every one with these bloody heals on this shiny, slippy floor!

Mo sees me and quickly brings over a young waiter who he says will look after me tonight, a slight inward giggle and raise of the eyebrow and before you know it, I'm whisked off to a prime positioned table just for one.

So, I forgot to mention, Mo and in fact all the staff in this luxury hotel are forbidden to have relations with any of the guest or they will lose their job, which is a shame as I have a huge double bed in my room which seems such a waste.

After 15 or so minutes a very large smiley Egyptian man came and sat himself down telling me he was staying in the hotel alone as he was on a business trip. He was very jolly but not my type and I was a little worried what Mo might think? I needn't have worried as within minutes the young waiter was at my side asking if he was bothering me? I said I didn't want to be rude and excused myself to go to the ladies, on my return, he was gone.

On the short walk back from the bathroom I opened the swinging door straight into a guy and nearly sent him flying "Oh my gosh I'm so sorry "I am so clumsy sometimes it's embarrassing! The guy looked at me and smiled and said "wow you are beautiful" I blushed a little as my eyes glanced over the muscles trying to escape his t-shirt and his …eerm yes his eyes were lovely! I hurried off and sat down slightly flushed by the encounter. I don't normally go for muscle men, but I could make an exception for that one.

I turn around to look around the room, I can't believe it muscle man is heading in my direction with two drinks, one a red wine that I have been drinking this evening, is he coming to me? Surly not I look behind me but there is no one there, oh my, he sits down in the chair next to me and says, "why are you alone?" My heart is beating so fast, he is absolutely gorgeous and not to young! Apparently, he is also here on business, I didn't catch the details, I just couldn't concentrate I could feel my cheeks filling with colour and my pants getting damp and this time it wasn't my weak bladder failing me. He goes on to tell me that I have the perfect woman's body that he would love to explore! Oh my! I'm far from perfect at a rather short 5 ft nothing and size 14 with 38 E bust I have lumps and but apparently according to this guy its perfect as it is! Oh he's a charmer alright and he is good at it, he has a lovely room all to himself, oh I am so tempted but I can feel the watchful eyes of Mo and his staff on me, this one will have to wait, hopefully I will catch him by the pool tomorrow, I don't want to let him go but even I can't be so brazen. I excuse myself and head to the bathroom again, just one of the joys of getting older and having given birth three times. The only plus side to having a slight prolapse is that guys always say I'm really tight, who am I to tell them that actually it's my prolapsed bladder squashing their somewhat disappointing penis.

As I suspected as I returned, he was gone. I decided as it was getting late, and I'd been travelling all day that I would go and get cosy in my room so that I'm fresh for tomorrow. Just as I stood to leave Mo came over and whispered "I'm going for a shower then I will meet you" then he was gone! Meet me where? What? No, I've got my big pants on!! Shit! I dash back to my room to freshen up and change into sexy undies that I had bought especially for this holiday.

I'd only been in my room a few mins when I received a text saying meet me at the coffee shop, Coffee shop. What coffee shop? I can't just walk down the street on my own!   On the second text, He gave me directions and said leave now and I will meet you.

I think the booze must have gone to my head because before I knew it I was out of the hotel and halfway down the road. Well girls have needs too! And it has been a while!

My heart is pounding, and I feel sick, what am I doing?? You hear the stories of these stupid women wondering off on their own in foreign countries… and here I am! What an idiot!! How stupid am I! Just then I see Mo, phew was I glad to see him. He hurries me along and off the main road, "where are we going?" I ask. "Quickly to the apartment we can't be seen" he replied couldn't decide if I was excited, nervous, or just absolutely shitting myself! The apartment was in fact not an apartment but a disused derelict hotel. AS we walked over my heart was pounding, what if there were other men waiting inside? You hear so many stories of gang rape and sex slavery, what if I'm to spend the rest of my holiday chained up in this hell hole being raped rather than sunning myself in luxury. I tell myself I've watched to many films, and unfortunately even if that were to happen, Liam Neason wouldn't be rescuing me anytime soon.

I was relieved when Mo opened the door to reveal that 'the apartment' say that in very loose terms was in fact empty. This relief was short lived when I looked around and saw the state of the place. There was a thread bare sofa that looked like it may be infested with all kinds of creatures, a toilet but no loo roll and in another room a bed that actually looked ok, but not exactly inviting.

I was led straight to the bedroom.......

I wasn't expecting to be wooed and romanced, I thought the reality would be fast and furious, hot, and steamy tearing at each other's clothes, passionate fucking, I can't get enough of you kind of fuck, hot and sweaty naughty but oh so nice!

Unfortunately, it was none of the above, well apart from the fast bit. If I said the sex that night was a bit like drive through fast food…It was quick and convenient but left you disappointed and still hungry.

It was all over before it began, there was no foreplay not even a spit n rub! I knew it wouldn't be amazing first time, but I wasn't prepared for this. He threw me on the bed pulled my pants off and then with one hand gripped firmly over my mouth pinning me to the bed he proceeded to pound me as hard as he could for all of about thirty seconds. When he then released a roar of ecstasy. Job done! He then lit a cigarette put his pants on and made it clear that was it for the evening. I was more than a little stunned, I don't mind a bit of rough sex, in fact it can be great fun, but this was bordering on rape. it's a shame because he is so cute looking and he has the equipment needed, he just needs to improve on technique. I don't think for one minute Mo thought anything was wrong, I honestly believe he was inexperienced, with pent up frustration and just culturally very different.

Well, I have two choices, I could just write this off and never come here again, plenty more fish and all or I could teach him how thigs should be done? I will put it down to first night nerves and give him another go, only next time I will take charge.

I put my knickers in my pocket and ran back to the hotel as quick as my short legs would take me, which wasn't very fast. I'm definitely going to have to start some sort of exercise/diet when I get home.

THE CLEANER

The next day I woke early with the sun streaming through the patio door's, last night feels like a hazy dream, I almost questioned if it actually happened, gosh I must have been more than a little tipsy? I brush this thought off, I'm on holiday and I'm here alone, I can do whatever I like.

It's 6:30 am and the sun is blazing in, and I can't bear to miss a second of it, so I jump in the shower then get out on the balcony to dry in the sun and start applying my sun lotion. I figured as it's so early and there aren't many people around I could just sit wrapped in a towel whist I do this.

I'm in my element. I love, love, love the sun especially the warm dapple effect on my face as it beams through the trees blowing in the breeze, I love peaceful mornings just listening to the birds and watching the morning prep around the pool. I start applying my array of creams, one just for the face as a red burnt nose is never attractive, one for my body that just smells lush like tropical fruit and then an any way up spray so that I can get my back, this is one of the problem's a lone traveller must consider. I treat this time not as a chore but like a mini relaxing spa massage enjoying every second of slowly massaging and the aroma of heavenly tropics, my towel kept slipping but I didn't worry as there was barely a soul around and to be honest, I'm not really that bothered if anyone does see.

I was lost in thought as I stood with one leg on the chair massaging cream into my thigh when I got that feeling that someone was watching me. I turned around and there on the next balcony was a very handsome cleaner watching my every move, so I did what any confident flirt would do... I squirted more cream on and slowly massaged it in whilst smiling at him as my towel began to slip. He didn't waiver! He held my stare and smiled back obviously enjoying the show. I thought hmmm interesting, he is cute looking, confident, and the only member of staff allowed in my room. Could I? Should I? Would I? I turned to look at him once more, but he was gone. I went inside to prep my bag for the day when I heard a knock at the door. It was the cleaner! OMG! I feel myself going pink! I'm not so brazen now he's stood right in front of me! Whilst I'm stood in nothing but a towel!!

He asks whether I could change some coins into a note for him. "Sure, come in" I said in a weird high pitch voice. My palms are sweating as I start fiddling with my purse, he stood there cool a s a cucumber, his deep brown eyes watching my every move (probably waiting for my towel to slip) I can see through his loose work trousers that he is pleased to see me as he unashamedly stands there with a clear erection! So many thoughts are going through my head right now, is he going to grab my towel and throw me on the bed and take me whether I want him to or not! Or am I being the sex crazed confident lone traveller going to make the first move? Only I'm not feeling so confident now. I handed him the £10 note he said thank you, then turned and walked out. I was relieved and I I'm honest a little disappointed. Oh well that sunshine is waiting for me I better get ready and get my spot by the pool.

OIL ME UP!

I decided I was going to sit by the pool that my balcony overlooked, there were a few reasons for this, one this is where Olivia and I spent most of our time so the staff know me already and make sure I am waited on, none of this waiving the waiter over, he just puts me a drink on very rotation, it's also near the snack bar should I get a little peckish, it's also one of the quieter pools as its more of a lazy river it doesn't lend itself to balls or kids being thrown around. But the main reason I chose this pool is that it's right by my room should I need anything, you know like a pooh! Ha ha I know you hear me, why is it we don't like to pooh in a public toilet? I mean after all, we all have to take a dump sometime yet we all, well most of us just don't want anyone else to know!

As I walked over the pool the guys spotted me and sprang into action positioning a bed and table in the prime position making sure that the bed is on an angle between the pool and some shrubbery to make the most of the all-day sunshine but more importantly making sure no one can come and sit to close. I never understand why people feel the need to encroach on my space, the Spanish are particularly bad for this noticed over the last few years of holidaying there. If you ever go to the beach in Spain you will see that its always around three umbrellas from the sea but there isn't an inch of spare sand in-between, several times I have rocked up and embarrassingly squeezed into a gap that I think is too small to find that within twenty minutes another two families with kids have come and joined me. I like to have a bit of room to spread out, I like my own company and don't feel the need to speak to every randomer. I get myself cosy headphones in podcast on, drink in hand, eyes closed, and I am in heaven!

As I open my eyes, I am greeted by a tall grey haired German man in the tiniest speedos leaning over me, I was a little startled to say the least as a hand was thrust forward and Hans from Berlin proceeded to introduce himself and then plonk himself rather familiarly on the end of my sun lounger. He talked none stop about how he had been married, now divorced, and loves holidaying alone he barely came up for air, I smiled and nodded in all the right places whilst trying to curl my toes up and away as Hans had nearly sat on them, and though I'm a modern girl I didn't quite fancy toeing Hans poolside for all to see.

I was lost in my own thoughts whilst trying to figure Hans out, he was probably late sixties maybe early seventies though well kept, he obviously worked out, I noticed he had his nipple pierced which I decided meant he had a rather kinky side, whilst I was lost in thought Hans bellowed at me "Katie will you put oil on me?"

OMG what did he say?! Surely not! how do I even reply? I want the ground to swallow me up as I feel everyone around the pool is watching and awaiting my response. Is this his chat up line? Am I supposed to ask him to return the favour? Does he mean just apply the oil or is he expecting a full-on sexy massage? After rather long and awkward pause I smile and replied "Sure" I'm thinking he will mean later on, by which time I will be able to sneak away pretending to go to lunch or something.

But NO! To my horror Hans magically produced a bottle of oil, God only knows where that came from as those budgie smugglers didn't have room for pockets. Hans handed me the oil then straddled my lounger so that his back was facing me and the shouted "come, Katie come" waiving to his back. I couldn't help but giggle at the absurdity of this scenario, a strange older German guy ordering me to come on his back! Ha-ha, it will take a little more than rubbing oil on his wrinkly skin to make me come!

I decided to just get it over with as quick as possible, but as I poured the oil into my hands I glance up and see my cleaner glaring down at me from my balcony. That wicked side of my just can't contain itself! Staring back at my horny cleaner I start to give Hans the massage of his life. I pulled up close with my legs spread around him, with every upward stroke I heaved my heavy breast up close so that my nipples skimmed across his back the moves were slow and sensual my breathing heavy, I can hear little moans coming from Hans, I look up to my balcony, my gorgeous cleaner is still there watching and smiling, he obviously knows that this show is for his benefit. Then he pulls something from his pocket and holds it to his face, I can't quite make it out, and then he waves, OMG it's my knickers! The sexy ones I had on last night! I started laughing and slapped Hans on the back to signal that his fun was over. Poor Hans scurried off with nowhere to hide his protruding man hood, well that will teach him to wear such offensive swim wear.

CHOPSTICKS

M o had been messaging all day, but I stayed rather aloof with my replies, I had booked myself into one of the oriental al la carte restaurants for dinner, Liv and I had eaten there last time and the food was exceptional, and Chef Alli had taken a shine to me, so I was looking forward to surprising him. I dressed in a black leather pencil skirt, a slouchy of the shoulder grey T-shirt, nude kitten heals and lots of chunky silver jewellery. I looked and felt great, sexy, sassy, and confident but with a relaxed, easy not tried to hard look.

Chef Alli saw me approaching and bounded over like a love-struck puppy, he threw his arms around me and nearly squeezed the life out of me!

"Why did you not tell me you were coming?" He said.

Then he ushered me in and told me I would eat nothing but the best, he was going to prepare a banquet fit for a queen just for me! Ha-ha I love all this attention. The waiters never stop bringing me water, wine and probably every item from the menu! There was sushi, won ton, soup, dishes with prawns, lobster, beef, noodles, and rice, I couldn't have possibly eaten it all, but I loved the fuss and trying all the different delicacies. I could feel the other diner's eyes on me as the dishes and wine kept flowing to my table. It would seem everyone else had a set menu of just one starter, a main and a dessert. No one else was getting this five-star treatment. I didn't stuff my face with all the food I literally just had a mouthful of everything but I sat there and slowly enjoyed the food the attention and the people watching.

Have you ever been embarrassed to be British? This was one of those cringe moments. Sat opposite me was a table of six elderly Brits, it's always amusing watching the dynamics of relationships. There was one couple out of the six that obviously thought they were better, more well-travelled and much more confident than the other four, the guy in this couple had decided that he was the alpha male, he was ordering the wine and choosing what everyone should eat in a rather loud voice. When their food arrived, he proudly announced that he and his wife always eat with chopstick. He was bellowing "when in Rome and all that" this alone made me laugh, because you're not in Rome, you in an Asian inspired restaurant run by Egyptians in Egypt! He looked at his wife who then rather nervously picked up her chopsticks and then they both started to eat with their chopsticks.

Now don't get me wrong, I love chopsticks and do myself use them. But these two plonkers hadn't snapped the chopsticks before using them. You know how sometimes they come joined together and you gently snap them to release them, well these two didn't, so then proceeded to stab at their food! Plates were banging and food was flying off as both were stabbing away as he continued to tell the rest of the table how he always uses chopsticks, only these Egyptian ones are a little more difficult due to the fact that they are stuck together!!!! Oh, my day's I can hardly breath I'm laughing so much. In the end I don't know who looked the craziest, them and their stabbing sticks or me sat alone crying with laughter!

I snuck out before Chef Alli could get to me and went to the ladies to fix my make-up. I walked into Mo's bar knowing I looked great, as I did the young boy came over to usher me to my table, but I had other plans, I told him I was fine and that I wouldn't be staying, I ordered a tequila at the bar, downed it in one and sashayed out with a smile. I could feel Mo's eyes on me as I walked out, but I wasn't going to give him the satisfaction of telling him my plans for the rest of the evening. My only plan that evening was to get into bed alone and watch a movie, but he didn't need to know that I got into my beautiful big bed and switched my phone on silent, I won't be replying to any of his messages till tomorrow.

Morning routine

There seems to be only one plug socket that my adapter fits in and it's on the opposite side of the room to my bed. I like to sleep with my phone right next to me, in case of emergencies, I'm not quite sure what emergency that might be but the way this adventure is going, it's probably best to be on the safe side. Because of this my phone has barely any battery by morning so I need time to charge it. This s fine because I get up at the first crack of sunlight probably due to the fact that I sleep with the curtains open so that the sun floods in and I'm in no danger of missing any of that glorious warmth on my body. You could say I'm a bit of a sun worshiper, well all I can say is anyone that stand's and blocks my sun will feel my wrath, as many friends have realised. I have a little routine going on in the morning of prepping myself for the day ahead. Firstly, I jump in the shower and exfoliate and shave, preparation is key to good tanning and hair grows with the grass in this heat, no one wants spider's legs hanging out of there bikini. I always use that fresh tingling tea-tree shower gel on holiday my thinking is that because it goes so cold on the skin it keeps you cooler for longer and therefor helps keep sweating to a minimum.

have no actual proof that this happens, but it makes sense in my head. I then put the kettle on and make .... a cup-a-soup!! Oh, I know it's wrong and it should be tea, but this way I feel like I've had a hot drink and breakfast combined saving me valuable sunbathing time. I take my soup out onto the balcony and start applying my lotions and potions whilst the cleaner again watches on adoringly, well maybe not adoringly? Maybe just horny?

Once I'm all oiled up I go into to let it all the creams soak in and start to apply my face. Just because I'm on my hols in blistering heat doesn't mean I can't put a bit of effort in! I first apply my 48hour eyebrow gel, it's a thick gloopy gel that you paint over eyebrows and around fifteen mins later peel off to reveal beautiful brows that won't smudge when my face sweats with the blistering heat. A sweep of waterproof mascara to make the eyes pop! Next a little ruby woo lip, as you are never dressed without it! I truly believe the red lip makes a bare face look made-up! I finish with big hoop earrings, and decide which of my over large sunnies I want to wear today? A big spray of coco, I'm not dressed without it! And then its outfit time!

So many women overlook the importance of day wear on holiday, choosing to throw on a big T-shirt or Kaftan that does nothing for the figure and hides most of the flesh that wants tanning!

I have THE PERFECT summer dress! It's a pretty pale blue soft but heavy cotton with pockets.

Pockets are just the best!! Its strapless so I won't get any strap marks whilst wandering around this huge hotel, across the top (breast area) it has a huge frill that means I can go braless!! Any girls with heavy titties like me will understand the value of this! The fabric skims rather than hugs, it is just past the knee hiding my fat unsightly varicose vein filled knees but shows of my slimmer calf, the material is light enough to be cool but heavy enough not to blow up in the slightest breeze. I give my hair a shake to give it a little volume, I always wear it down as think its sexier having hair swishing around that I can twiddle with. I lip on my pretty sparkling flip flops and off I go.....

I have decided to adventure off to another pool just in case Hans i
lurking nearby, I'm really not in the mood for men today, an
especially not old wrinklies in speedos!!

I wander around the grounds and its seventeen swimming pools! Mos
of the brits seem to hang around the active pool where there is music
aqua aerobics, and lots of people with bad tattoos. Don't get me wron;
I have a couple of tattoos myself, but I designed them myself I didn'
get them off Pinterest or worse still a tattoo parlours book in Benidorm

No, the action pool is not for me, I can't cope with the animation tear
constantly mithering to get me to play darts or do yoga and no I won'
dress up in a giant bear suit for the kids!!!!! So, I wander a little furthe
and find the perfect spot! A large pool with fixed sunbeds, none of the
dragging beds around and getting too close for comfort malarkey,
large poolside bar and restaurant, several snack and ice cream bars
waiter service and toilets and showers with a fresh towel hut
PERFECT!

I unpack my bag and get set up and then go to the ladies to pop on m
bikini, well no one knows me, and these Egyptians seem to like a fev
curves, plus confidence is the most attractive thing a woman can wear.

As I come out of the changing room, I go over to the mirror to check a
is in its right place, and OMG!!!! My eyebrows!!! I have forgotten t
take off my tattoo gel!!!!! I have just sashayed around this hotel wit
giant black eyebrows! Jheeeze! I hope my sunglasses covered them!!
compose myself once more double check nothing else is a miss an
head back to my lounger.

Usually, I would drink my water and maybe a beer or two in the earlie
part of the day but today after the whole Mo crappy sex thing and th
eyebrows trauma, when the waiter came by, I decided stuff it! I'm o
holiday I don't have to answer to anyone, I'm having a large G & T.

Several drinks later …….

The pool area was fairly quiet, with most people having gone off fc
lunch, also this to my delight is an adult only area, so no screamin

30

whinging brats around splashing and just generally irritating me.

I do like children, just in very small doses. I loved my girls when they were little, in fact I was one of those annoying mums that would insist on taking my children everywhere including fancy restaurants and wine bars for lunch, I used to say, why shouldn't I? just because I have children doesn't mean I want to sit in a whacky warehouse!".

Now that my little darlings have all grown up, I absolutely despair at people like that! Leave the little shits at home and let us all have some peace. Peace is what I have right now, pure bliss, no music blaring, no kids screeching just the sound of my ice clinking as I drink my G & T, heaven.

I get engrossed in the book on my kindle, I had downloaded it thinking it was a light-hearted comedy, but it turned out to be a dark and twisted thriller, about a crazy female serial killer, I couldn't believe how easy it sounded to pop people off! One of her victim's had a nut allergy, so she put tiny traces of nuts in her water bottle! Evil genius! whilst reading I was thinking do I dislike anyone enough? Could I kill? I didn't come to a definite conclusion, there are many factors to consider.

Whilst my mind was wondering my eyes were getting heavy and I must have just slipped into a little snooze...

Have you ever seen films where women just close their eyes and drift serenely into sleep, then awaken looking just as perfect...how? I mean genuinely how do they do that?

I abruptly awoke due to me snoring so loud my whole body Had vibrated, it was like the sound of a herd of buffaloes crashing through the plains. I startled jumped so high I nearly fell off the bed! I could feel the sticky drool running down my face and neck, my sunglasses a squiff, my hair sweaty and sticking to my face, sweat was running from under my boobs, yep one big sweaty disorientated mess, nothing like the women in the films. And to top it all, I was no longer lying face down. The horror as I realised.

I had whilst reading turned on my front and undone my bra strap to avoid unsightly tan lines. But during my not so lady like snooze I had rolled over completely exposing my huge heavy and without a bra rather pendulous breasts, not only that but during my roll my bottoms had wedged up the crack of my bum pulling the pants across and exposing more flap than anyone one should ever see in daylight!

Yes, I had exposed myself poolside!!! As I try to come round I can here shouting, I look up to see the couple next to me, the guy is leering over grinning whilst his wife is whittering on waving her arms in my direction and occasionally slapping him, I have no idea what language they are speaking but I get the jist of what's being said, I smiled rather nonchalantly and readjusted myself. I went off to the bathroom splashed myself down, fixed myself up, checked all was in place and headed back to the pool, by the time I got back the couple had left, meaning I could resume relaxing without the hateful and lustful eyes upon me.

At this point I should have realised today is one of those days and gone and locked myself away before any real damage is done, but no, I just thought oh well what else could go wrong? And well, yes, I'm on my holiday and nobody knows me, I have no one to answer to so stuff it!

Then standing in front of my was this very beautiful tall, dark, handsome waiter with a G & T and a smile, he introduced himself though I didn't catch his name as I was lost in his deep brown eyes, I had to almost pinch myself he was so gorgeous, he sat down on the end of the lounger and started talking to me about England, which part I was from and how he had lived in England for 18 months, I wasn't really listening, I just smiled and nodded, then he got up and said he must get back to work and he was gone.

I needn't have worried though, for before I was halfway through my drink, he was back with a fresh one. By the third or fourth drink I was a little more, relaxed shall we say? We were chatting and giggling, then he said "I will take you out tonight, I will pick you up outside the hotel in a taxi at 8pm" before I knew it, we had exchanged numbers and he was gone. I looked at the time, oh my where does time go? It was 6:30

already I hurry back to the room to get ready.

Back at the room I had a quick shower, threw on a cute but rather short floaty number, some ankle tie wedges, and I was good to go! A good spritz of Channel and off I went.

As I hurried out of the hotel and into the awaiting taxi I could feel the eyes on me (Mo had staff everywhere watching my every move).

I was greeted in the taxi by a beautiful smiling *boy*, oh my days what had I been thinking? He was so YOUNG! I must have been really pissed this afternoon! I'm looking at this boy, he could only be 20years old, which is a year younger than my eldest daughter! As we start to pull away, I said "I'm sorry, this is a mistake, I need to go back". He tried to calm me, saying its ok we are just friends we will go for one drink, then if you still want to go, I will take you back, no problem. I have no idea why I agreed, I should have got out there and then, but I stupidly agreed to go for one drink.

We arrived at a seedy looking bar, he ushered me in and sat me in a corner, and went to the bar, he came back with two drinks, a milkshake for him and a gin & tonic for me. A milkshake! I know locals are not supposed to drink, but he could have got a coke or something. I sit there drinking my drink thinking how the hell do I get out of this situation? I looked at my phone, SHIT no service! As I'm looking at my phone his hand slides up my inner thigh, "WTF are you doing!" I pushed his hand away and stood to my feet, as I did I began to sway, my head was spinning, I felt so disorientated, I collapsed back onto the sofa, for a few minutes I couldn't figure out what was happening, I can't be drunk I've not even finished my drink, I know I had a lot today, but I had at least a two hour gap whilst getting ready, I'm trying so hard to work out what's going on, I feel almost paralyzed, I can hear noises, people talking, music, I can feel hands running up my thighs trying feverishly to get into my pants.

was drifting into a state of unconsciousness, I tried to fight it with all my might, I pushed his hands off me and forced myself up on to my feet, but I had no control over my body, my legs were weak and felt almost like I had pins and needles in them, I tried to step away, but I stumbled and fell.

The boy was quickly helping me to my feet, saying he would look after me. It was then I realised, he must have drugged me! Whilst at the bar he must have slipped something into my drink. At that moment I didn't have the strength to do anything, I vaguely remember him helping me into an awaiting car and then I passed out.

Maybe this is a regular occurrence, maybe the taxi driver, the bar man and the boy all work together, maybe there are more of them, as I slip in and out of consciousness I can feel him all over me, the pain as he squeezes and bites my breast, one of his hands has made it into my pants whilst the other is tugging at his belt trying to release himself. I'm willing myself to wake from this nightmare. Come on wake up, wake up! Even in this drugged up state I am aware that situation is only going to get worse, I have no idea what fate lies ahead, but I know it's not going to be good. Then the sound of sirens and flashing lights are all around, I'm so confused? The boy straightened me up and said in a panic-stricken voice, "you have to say you are my wife! This is not allowed". He got out of the car, then there was a bang on the window, a gun bearing police officer was screaming at me and waving his machine gun, I thought I'm going to throw up! What the hell is happening? And what is going to happen to me? Oh my God! What if I end up in an Egyptian jail? No one knows I am even outside of the hotel. I could be gone for days before anyone would raise the alarm. So many terrifying scenarios are running through my head, what are my poor girls going to do? How will they cope without me? Will they start a campaign to free me? Am I going to be Stockport's answer to Deirdre Barlow, Free the Weatherfield one! Back in coronation street.

The driver puts the window down as the police officer is shouting at me "papers" I am trying so hard to focus and comprehend what he' saying, I cry out "I'm English, hotel Jazz" I open my bag to see if I hae ID, but I have nothing!! How fucking stupid am I; no one knows I'r here, I have no ID and no phone signal! I think I'm gonna hurl out of this window and cover this police officer in puke! Then I would probably be done for assault on top of everything.

Then just like that it was over, the boy got back in the taxi, and we drove away. I have no idea even to this day what happened, and I really don't care, the car drove in the direction of the hotel, as soon as I could see the lights lighting up the gardens and the hotel sign, I threw myself out of the moving car and ran! Luckily the drugs had started to wear off, probably due to the fear and the adrenalin cursing threw my veins. I ran as fast as I could without stopping till I got into my hotel room. I locked the door behind me and then dragged the desk across the room and pushed it up to the door. I ran into the bathroom and threw my guts up.

BEER FEAR & ANXIETY

Have you ever had beer fear? I don't get it often, but this day it was real and crippling. My head was still spinning with last night's shenanigans. I still felt sick, I looked shocking, my face was a mess with mascara tears running down my face, I was so pale I looked like a vampire had visited me in the night, I had teeth marks and bruises on my breasts, and I felt so very very ashamed, embarrassed, and stupid, how could I at my age, get into such a dangerous predicament?

I decide I must pull myself together, as terrifying as last night was, I can't let it eat me up, I need to just take it on the chin and hopefully learn from the stupid and irresponsible mistakes I have made.

I get myself beach ready, today I do not want and poolside drama, I want the peace and tranquillity of an empty beach with nothing but the sound of the waves lapping at my feet.

I put on the biggest sunnies I can find and a big floppy hat and walk the back way to the beach hoping no one sees me.

Whilst at the beach I thought about whether I should try to press charges or complain to the hotel staff management about the boy and last night's dramas, but I decided that I didn't want to get embroiled in anymore dramas, and at the end of the day it was my own stupid fault for being so naive. Oh, I know, some would say I should pursue the matter and prevent others from getting into such a scary situation but if I'm truly honest, I just don't want to, I am emotionally and physically battered and bruised, and I just want to forget everything!! Head in the sand is exactly what I want right now. I get set up and settle in on a four-poster beach bed and fall asleep, absolutely exhausted.

I woke up around 2pm absolutely starving! Hangover hunger has kicked in. I go to the beach bar and order virtually everything on the menu, pizza, chips, salad a burger and a pint of lager to wash it down, hair of the dog and all that. I started to feel so much better. I decided I would have another couple of beers whilst people watching.

I am always highly amused when people watching, I wonder what goes through their minds when they look in the mirror, surely their friends, partners or whoever they are with, must say something? Oh, and I'm not body shaming, just style shaming. I know plenty larger women that know exactly how to dress themselves and look stunningly fabulous. But I am sat in a beach bar serving food, isn't there a dress code? Honestly, I do not want to see someone's intimate bits n bobs whilst I'm eating. Why do some women class a see through mesh dress a cover-up? It covers nothing! I can see your tities jiggle and don't even let me start on the eyeful I got when you leant across the table for the salt! Then there's a woman sat with a coat on, it's thirty degrees love!! Honestly you do not need a coat. There's another woman that's had her hair braided, and all in between her braids her scalp is burnt and bright red and looks excruciatingly painful but even that doesn't distract me from the orange neon fringed T-shirt that says "I heart Benidorm" on the front. The men are no better, one in itsy bitsy speedos with beer belly and so much back hair, he could have gone with Ms I love Benidorm and had it braided. Another guy with ¾ length pant on and a vest, dear lord! What is wrong with you? ¾ length pants have or at least should never have been a thing, and vest's no no no no no! unless you look like David Beckham, you should never wear a vest! I decided this is more than enough entertainment for one day and head back to my room for a movie and an early night, yesterday's dramas have been put to bed and tomorrow is a new day.

TOWELGATE

Have you ever stayed in a hotel where the maids arrange towels and petals on the bed into heart shapes, well this hotel did just that, only as time has gone on the towels are less like flowers and hearts and more like giant phallic objects or voo doo doll contortionist. I feel like my sexy cleaner is trying to tell me the story of what he'd like to do to me through his towel art.

Yesterday I walked in to find a towel person, on all fours, he had even adorned it with my own earrings and had carefully placed a flower over what would be the butt hole! I mean he is a very talented towel artist, but I'm not quite sure how to take it.

Its kind of flattering in a very bazar way.

No More Mo

I have been avoiding Mo and his text messages, initially I had thought about potentially revisiting him, and even showing him a thing or two, but my brush with the law has really spooked me.

My holiday is quickly coming to an end, and if I am honest I will be glad to get home, no more Mo, no more crazy shenanigans, I just need to get home safely.

My time in Egypt has been filled with excitement and well, FEAR! Haha.

I think next time I go away I might go to a slightly more liberal country.

So where shall I go next?

Printed in Great Britain
by Amazon

19861037R00031